Dear Parents:

Congratulations! Your child is taking the first steps on an exciting journey. The destination? Independent reading!

STEP INTO READING® will help your child get there. The program offers five steps to reading success. Each step includes fun stories and colorful art or photographs. In addition to original fiction and books with favorite characters, there are Step into Reading Non-Fiction Readers, Phonics Readers and Boxed Sets, Sticker Readers, and Comic Readers—a complete literacy program with something to interest every child.

Learning to Read, Step by Step!

Ready to Read   Preschool–Kindergarten
• big type and easy words • rhyme and rhythm • picture clues
For children who know the alphabet and are eager to begin reading.

Reading with Help   Preschool–Grade 1
• basic vocabulary • short sentences • simple stories
For children who recognize familiar words and sound out new words with help.

Reading on Your Own   Grades 1–3
• engaging characters • easy-to-follow plots • popular topics
For children who are ready to read on their own.

Reading Paragraphs   Grades 2–3
• challenging vocabulary • short paragraphs • exciting stories
For newly independent readers who read simple sentences with confidence.

Ready for Chapters   Grades 2–4
• chapters • longer paragraphs • full-color art
For children who want to take the plunge into chapter books but still like colorful pictures.

STEP INTO READING® is designed to give every child a successful reading experience. The grade levels are only guides; children will progress through the steps at their own speed, developing confidence in their reading.

Remember, a lifetime love of reading starts with a single step!

Step into Reading, Random House, and the Random House colophon are registered trademarks of Penguin Random House LLC.

Visit us on the Web!
StepIntoReading.com
rhcbooks.com

Educators and librarians, for a variety of teaching tools, visit us at RHTeachersLibrarians.com

ISBN 978-0-7364-3857-5 (trade) — ISBN 978-0-7364-8262-2 (lib. bdg.)
ISBN 978-0-7364-3858-2 (ebook)

Printed in the United States of America   10 9 8 7 6 5 4 3 2 1

Disney · PIXAR

INCREDIBLES 2

THE
INCREDIBLE
ELASTIGIRL

by Natasha Bouchard

illustrated by the Disney Storybook Art Team

Random House 🏠 New York

Helen Parr is a Super
called Elastigirl.
She can stretch, bend, and twist
into any shape.
Her husband
is Mr. Incredible.
He is a Super, too.

With their family,
they battle
the Underminer,
an evil villain.
The Underminer tries
to destroy the city.

The Underminer steals money
from the banks.
The Supers try to stop him,
but he gets away.

The Underminer
has left a big mess.
The city is ruined!
Everyone blames the Supers.

The Supers' agency
is shut down.
Supers are illegal.
The Parr family must find
a new place to live.

Winston Deavor is a rich man.

He wants to help Mr. Incredible,

Elastigirl, and their friend Frozone.

He wants to show the public

that the city needs Supers.

His sister, Evelyn, built
a special camera
for the Supersuits.
It will film the Supers
in action.

Winston lets the Parr family live
in one of his many homes.
The huge house is full
of waterfalls and pools!

Elastigirl gets the first job.

She puts on her new Supersuit.

She gets on her bike.

Mr. Incredible will stay home
with Jack-Jack, Violet,
and Dash.

Elastigirl speeds after
a runaway train.
She must save the train
before it crashes.

Elastigirl stops the train
just in time!
The villain Screenslaver
wanted it to crash.

Elastigirl is a hero
for saving the train.
She is excited!
She tells Mr. Incredible
about her mission.

Mr. Incredible watches Elastigirl
on every news channel.
The public loves her!

The Screenslaver
has captured
an important ambassador!
Elastigirl leaps to a helicopter.
She saves the ambassador!

Elastigirl uses a special device
to track down the Screenslaver.
She blows up
like a parachute.
She catches the villain!

But something
does not feel right.
Elastigirl checks the camera
on her suit.
She zooms in.

Evelyn is worried.

Elastigirl has seen too much.

Evelyn is the Screenslaver!

She hypnotizes Elastigirl

with her hypno-goggles.

Evelyn is working

against the Supers.

Elastigirl tries

to break free,

but she cannot move.

Meanwhile,
Winston's plan
is working.
World leaders
make Supers legal again.

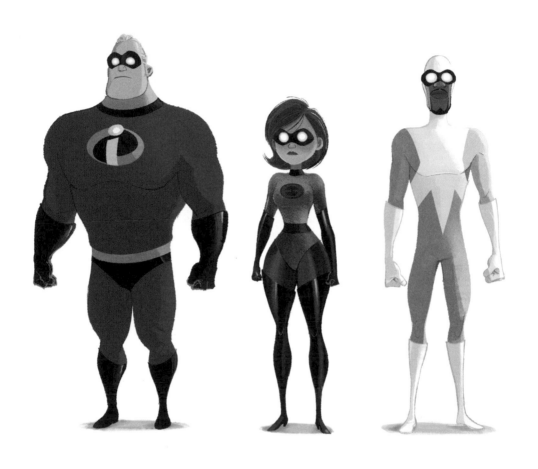

Evelyn wants to stop them.

She tricks Mr. Incredible.

She hypnotizes him
and Frozone, too.

Just then,

Violet, Dash,

and Jack-Jack arrive!

Jack-Jack pulls the hypno-goggles

off Elastigirl.

Elastigirl fights Evelyn.

Elastigirl stops Evelyn!

The police arrest her.

The Supers save the city

and become legal again!

Thanks to Elastigirl,

Supers will keep the city safe!

BORN **FAST**

INCREDIBLE **DAD**

INCREDIBLE **MOM**

INCREDIBLES 2

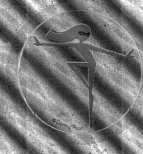

DASH

MR. TOUGH GUY

MOM TO THE RESCUE

FAMILY Dynamic